The Incredible Present

Harriet Castor

Adapted by Lesley Sims

Illustrated by Norman Young

Reading Consultant: Alison Kelly
Roehampton University of Surrey

Contents

Chapter 1

Lily

Lily Mack lived in a tall, old house
with her parents and her granny.
But most of the time it was just
Lily and Granny.

5

Lily's parents weren't like other parents. They always had some crazy project underway.

Their latest plan was to follow in the footsteps of the explorer, Monty Thripps. One hundred years ago, he had set off for the South Pacific in his balloon.

Mr. and Mrs. Mack had read about him in an old book. Then they had bought a balloon, packed their things and set off.

It was Lily's birthday tomorrow and there was no sign of Mr. and Mrs. Mack. Lily missed them a lot.

Granny was kind and funny – if a little forgetful. She and Lily did everything together. But it wasn't the same.

Lily decided to stop thinking about her parents and think about her birthday presents instead.

Her friend Freddy had a toy garage for his birthday. Lily enjoyed playing with it... but she didn't want a garage.

What about a giraffe? That
would be an amazing present.
Granny could knit a scarf to keep
it warm. But it might miss home.

A sky-gazing, star-seeking, shiny black telescope would be fun. She could go outside and look for Mars.

"I wonder if I'll get a telescope," Lily said. Granny put down her knitting and smiled.

"Wait until tomorrow," she said.

Chapter 2

A present hunt

At last, it was Lily's birthday
morning. She threw back her
covers and jumped out of bed.

Everything went flying as she threw on her clothes. Time for her presents!

Lily's friends had their presents at the breakfast table – not Lily. Each year, Granny put them in a different place.

Where would they be this year? Lily raced downstairs. A balloon was tied to the bannister.

Lily saw a note attached. A clue to her presents! She read it.

Happy
Birthday Lily.
Follow the arrow to
find your presents.

Where was the first arrow?
Lily looked down and spotted
it right away.

The trail took her all over the
tall, old house.

She saw spiders on
the stairway and
beetles in the
bathroom, but
she couldn't
see any
presents.

She looked
under the beds
and behind the
books. She still
couldn't find
any presents.

At last, she reached the sitting room. There sat Granny, knitting what would probably become the longest scarf in the world.

And there, in a corner of the sitting room, sat...

My presents!

Lily looked at her presents. What could be inside those three boxes?

Lily squished them and she squeezed them.

She stood them in a row...

...and
then
she
piled
them
high.

Finally, she read the labels
on each present to see who they
were from.

To Lily
love from
Cousin Jo

Happy Birthday Lily!
Love Aunty Alice
and Uncle Bob

lots of love
Granny x

Lily tore the paper off the present with the blue bow. But it wasn't a sky-gazing, star-seeking, shiny black telescope.

"Oh," said Lily. "Well, I suppose it was nice of Aunty Alice to remember my birthday."

And she still had two presents left. Lily opened the present with the green bow.

Sweet Wiff soap

But it wasn't a giraffe. It was a basket of smelly soap.

"Thank you Granny," said Lily.

23

Lily sighed. She only had one present left. Slowly, she unwrapped the present with the yellow bow.

"A box of writing paper!
Very useful," said Granny.
"Yes," said Lily.

Then she saw one last present...

To Lily
The Tall House
Blissop
(from somewhere
in the South Pacif

...from her parents.

Chapter 3

The last present

Lily looked at the brown parcel
and wondered what was inside.
Her parents always found
incredible presents.

Maybe it would be...

...a dinosaur tooth!

Or perhaps a rainbow
hamster?

Or even
an ice cream
plant (with
chocolate,
strawberry
and vanilla
flowers).

Lily held her breath. Slowly...
very slowly, she opened her
last present.

Inside was a small bag with
a label on it.

The Anything Bag.
Ask for anything
you want, reach
inside and there it
will be!

Anything? Anything at all?
Lily didn't know what to ask for
first. Perhaps she should start with
something small.

Lily reached into the bag. Sure enough, there was a box of six crayons.

Lily found some paper and sat down to try out the crayons...

...but she soon discovered something strange about them.

When she had finished
her pictures, Lily wrote a list
of everything she wanted to
ask the bag.

She forgot all about the
telescope. Who'd ask for a
telescope when they could
have *anything?*

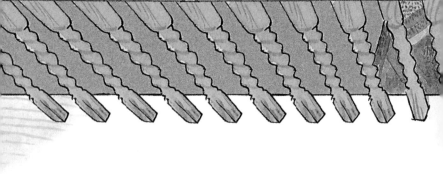

The list took her almost until
lunchtime. Then, Lily noticed
a second label on the bag...

Pet snail
Bubble bath with the biggest bubbles in the world

55 Bowls of pink icing

P. S. You can only ask for six things

P. S. You can only ask for six things

Oh squiddle! If she could only ask for six things, she had just five choices left.

She looked at her list and wondered what to choose.

Chapter 4

Three wishes

At the top of the list was a bed-making robot. Lily hated making her bed every morning.

Lily made her wish and reached
into the bag...

A bed-making robot please, bag!

...but the robot didn't do exactly what Lily had in mind.

Lily tried again. Next on her list was a space buggy. She could explore places no one else had seen.

Lily made her wish and reached into the bag...

With a flash and a bang there in front of her stood...

"Oh no!" cried Lily.

She had a space buggy, no doubt about it...

...but not exactly the space buggy she wanted.

So, Lily made another wish — for some magic of her own.

I'd like a witch's kit with real spells in it, please!

But the bag didn't hear her properly. Instead of a witch's kit with real spells in it...

...Lily got a witch's cat with real smells in it. It was hard to say who looked more surprised.

Things were not working out very well.

Just then, Granny called. "Lily! Lunchtime!"

Lily wrinkled her nose. "You stay here Cat," she said. "I'll bring you some food."

As she went downstairs, she wondered what Granny had cooked for her birthday lunch.

Chapter 5

The chocolate wish

It is spinach you like, isn't it, Lily?

Spinach? Why had Granny cooked spinach for her birthday lunch? Bleurch!

Lily didn't really mind spinach.
But it wasn't birthday food.
Birthday food should be special.

Quickly, she picked up the
bag and wished for...

A zapper that
turns all your greens
into chocolate
ice cream!

In a shower of stars, Lily pulled
the zapper out of her bag.

Lily pointed its enormous
hand at her plate of soggy,
green spinach and...

...zapped!

It worked! But not just on the spinach. Every single green thing had become chocolate ice cream.

48

"Lily, do something!"
cried Granny.

Ugh!
Help!

Chapter 6

Help!

Lily didn't know what to do.
If only her parents were home.

Then she thought of her bag.
Of course! She could ask the bag
to get them. She held it up.

Please bring them
home, bag... As quickly
as you can!

They arrived in a flash and still dressed up like explorers.

Lily began to tell them what had happened.

She told them about the robot
that made beds.

She told them about the
space buggy.

She was
telling them
about the
smelly cat
when he
walked by.

"Pooh!" said her dad. "We must
sort things out."

We'd better
put the bag into
reverse.

He turned the bag
inside out. Then Mrs. Mack
said a funny sentence.

For you asked
Lily everything back
take please,
bag dear.

Lily held her breath. Everyone waited to see what would happen next.

In a second the grass was green again – and not only the grass.

Lily couldn't smell the cat
any more.

The robot and his beds had gone.

And she couldn't hear any alien
babies squawking. Things were
back to normal. Well, almost.

Chapter 7

Starting again

"Sorry about that!" Dad said to Lily. "The bag was our first invention. We've decided to be inventors from now on."

Lily let out a sigh. "Does that mean you're home to stay?" she asked.

"Yes!" said her mother.

Lily thought that was the best
birthday present she could have.
They had a huge picnic to celebrate
– with no spinach in sight.

You'd never have guessed from looking at the picnic party what a strange birthday it had been.

But Granny was never quite so fond of her green hat after that. It always made her ears a little sticky.

Try these other books in
Series Two:

The Fairground Ghost: When Jake
goes to the fair he wants a really
scary ride. But first, he has to teach
the fairground ghost a trick or two.

The Clumsy Crocodile: Cassy, the
clumsiest crocodile in town, is about
to start her new job – as a shop
assistant in a china department...

Designed by
Katarina Dragoslavić
and Maria Wheatley

This edition first published in 2002 by Usborne Publishing Ltd.,
Usborne House, 83-85 Saffron Hill, London EC1N 8RT, England.
www.usborne.com
Copyright © 2002, 1995, 1994 Usborne Publishing Ltd.